The Best Fairy Tales of Grimm

The Wolf and the Seven Kids	1
Rapunzel	25
Hansel and Gretel	49
Cinderella	73
Mother Hulda	97
Little Red Riding Hood	121
The Bremen Town Musicians	145
Sleeping Beauty	169
Snow White	193
Rumpelstiltskin	217

The Wolf and the Seven Kids

Once upon a time there was a goat who had seven little kids. One day she wanted to go to the market to buy food. So she called all seven to her and said: 'Listen dear children – and listen very carefully!' She remained silent to see if she had everyone's attention and then she continued: 'I have to go shopping. You mustn't open the door to anyone. There's a wicked wolf lurking near here. If he comes in, he will devour you all. The wretch often disguises himself, but you will know him at once by his rough voice and his black feet. If he knocks, keep the door tightly shut!' The kids said, 'Dear mother, we will take good care of ourselves; don't worry.'

It was not long before someone knocked at the door of the house and called: 'open the door, dear children, your mother is here, and she has brought something for each of you.' When the kids heard the deep voice, they remembered their mother's warning. From behind the locked door, they said to the wolf: 'We know who you are! You're the wolf! Our mother has a sweet gentle voice, not a deep nasty one like yours! Go away! We'll never open the door to you!' And though the wolf banged furiously on the door, the kids, though trembling with terror, refused to let him into the house, and so the door remained shut.

The wolf, because that's who really was knocking on the door, realised the little kids were more clever than he thought. He did not try again and returned to the woods. There he noticed a colony of honeybees and had an idea. He dashed off to the baker and bought a big cake dripping with honey. He hoped this would sweeten his voice. In fact, after eating it, his voice didn't sound quite so deep. Over and over again, he practised imitating Mother Goat's voice. You see, he'd heard it in the woods. When he felt certain he could easily be mistaken for Mother Goat herself, he rushed back to the house and the seven kids.

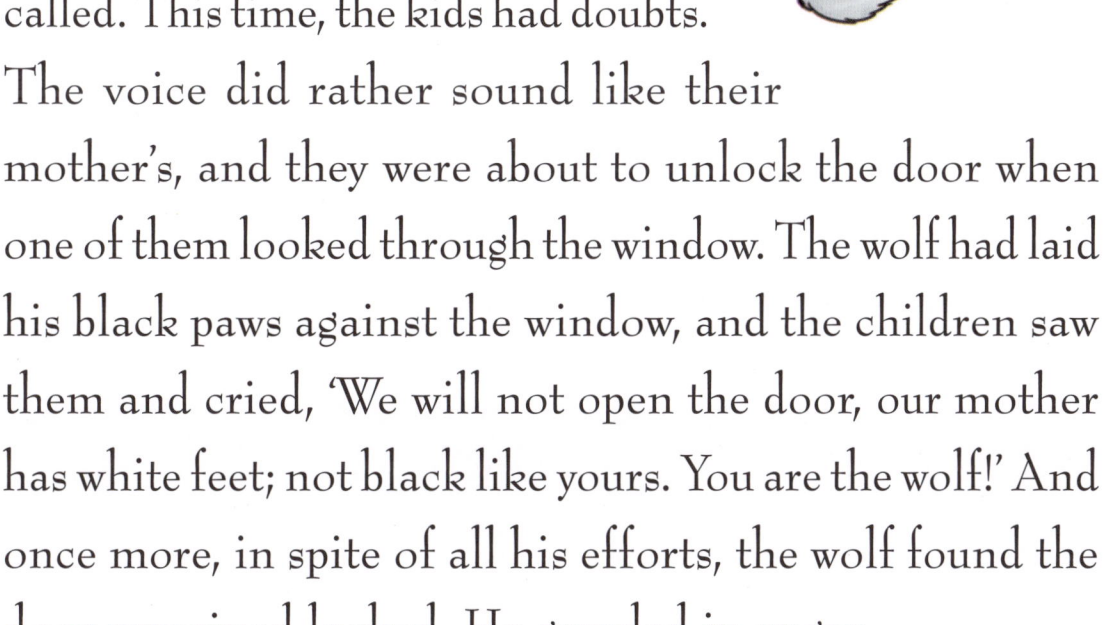

'Open the door! Open the door! It's Mother! I've just come back from the market and I have brought you delicious things! Open the door!' he called. This time, the kids had doubts. The voice did rather sound like their mother's, and they were about to unlock the door when one of them looked through the window. The wolf had laid his black paws against the window, and the children saw them and cried, 'We will not open the door, our mother has white feet; not black like yours. You are the wolf!' And once more, in spite of all his efforts, the wolf found the door remained locked. He growled in anger.

'You wait! I'll teach you,' the wolf said to himself. He ran down to the mill and asked the miller for a sack of flour. The miller hesitated. This wolf wants to deceive someone, he thought and he refused. But the shrewd wolf said, 'If you won't do it, I will devour you.' The miller was afraid, so he gave the wolf a whole sack of flour. The wolf at once jumped in it with his paws until all four were pure white. Very pleased with the result, he went off again to the goat's house. 'I'll trick them this time,' he said to himself. 'Mmm! I'm hungry! My tummy's so empty that my trousers are falling down! I'll swallow those tender kids whole!'

So the wretch went for the third time to the front door, knocked and said, 'Open the door for me, children. Your dear little mother has come home and has brought something from the forest for each one of you.' The voice sounded exactly like their mother's, but the wary kids quickly called out: 'Mother, let us see your feet because that bad wolf has already been here twice!' 'That's very good of you,' the wolf said in his sweetest voice. They peeked under door. When the kids saw the white feet, they believed everything he had said. The kids opened the door. But who should come in but the wolf! They were terrified and fled in all directions.

One leaped under the table, the second into the bed and the third into the stove, even though it was still hot. The fourth crouched in a barrel, the fifth in a cupboard, the sixth under the washing-bowl and the seventh hid in the grandfather clock. But the wicked wolf found the first six and swallowed them down, each with a single gulp. Inside the clock, the seventh little kid huddled, holding his breath as the wolf hunted down his brothers. He was the youngest and the only one to escape, for the wolf had satisfied his appetite. Weary, the wolf went off and laid down to sleep under a tree in the green meadow.

In the meantime, Mother Goat had come home. When she saw that the front door stood open, she rushed inside. She had a sinking feeling: what she feared had happened. Ah! What a sight greeted her: the table, chairs and benches were thrown around, the washing-bowl lay broken in pieces and the quilts and pillows were pulled off the bed! She searched for her children, but they were nowhere to be found. She called each of them in turn by name, but not one answered. At last, when she came to the youngest, she heard a soft crying from inside the clock. She called his name again. Open swung the clock door and out ran the little kid. Mother Goat held him in her arms while he told her the wolf had eaten all the others.

Stricken with grief, Mother Goat went out to the garden, and the youngest kid ran with her.

Suddenly, she heard a low wheezing sound: someone was snoring heavily. It was the greedy wolf, lying under a tree. His feast of kids had been too much for him and he was fast asleep. She looked at him from every side and saw that something was moving and struggling in his gorged belly. 'Ah, heavens', she said, 'is it possible that my poor children whom he has swallowed for his supper, can be still alive?' 'Hurry!' She said to the youngest, 'Run home and fetch me a needle and thread and a pair of scissors!'

Then Mother Goat cut open the wolf's stomach. Hardly had she made one cut, when one kid thrust its head out. She cut further and all six jumped out one after another. They had suffered no harm at all, for in his greediness the wolf had swallowed them down whole. What rejoicing there was! Mother Goat, however, said: 'Hurry! Hurry! Not a sound! We must get away before he wakes up! But first, fetch me some big stones! We will fill the wicked beast's stomach with them while he is still asleep.' The seven kids dragged the stones there as fast as they could. They put as many of them into his stomach as they could get in; and Mother Goat sewed him up again as quickly as possible, so that he was not aware of anything.

Later, the wolf woke with a raging thirst. 'What a heavy tummy I have!' he said. 'I've eaten too much! All those kids!' He went to the well to drink. When he bent down to get some water, his tummy full of stones tipped him over and he fell into the water. The weight took him straight to the bottom, and the goat and her kids shrieked with joy as he sank. 'The wolf is dead! The wolf is dead!' They danced for joy round about the well with their mother.

From that day on they all lived without fear of the wolf and for years to come, they told of their brave adventure about the wolf and the seven kids.

The End

Once upon a time there lived a man and a woman who were expecting a baby. They had a home next door to a witch called Gotel, whose splendid garden was surrounded by a high wall. From the couple's highest window, they could see this garden, full of the most beautiful flowers and herbs. One day, the woman saw a bed, stocked with rapunzel plants. They looked so fresh and green that she had the greatest desire to eat some. Every day her longing grew and she became very pale and thin. When her husband asked what was wrong, she replied: 'It's because of the rapunzel down there. If I can't eat some, I shall die'.

The man, who loved her so much, thought that sooner than let his wife die, he should bring her some of the rapunzel himself, no matter what the cost. He climbed over the wall, hastily clutched a handful of the plant and took it to his wife. She enjoyed it so much and it tasted so good that she longed for more. The husband hesitated, but the next evening he once again climbed into the garden. But there stood the witch, waiting for the thief who had stolen her rapunzel, threatening the poor man. 'Have mercy', he cried, 'my wife saw your rapunzel and felt such a longing for it that she would have died if she had not got some to eat'.

The witch allowed her anger to be softened, saying: 'From now on I will allow you to take as much rapunzel as you wish, but only on one condition: you must give me the child your wife will bring into the world. It shall be well treated, and I will care for it like a mother'. In his terror, the man consented. When the baby girl was born, the witch Gotel appeared and claimed the baby from the happy couple. She gave the child the name of Rapunzel, and took it away with her. By the age of twelve, Rapunzel was the most beautiful girl and Mother Gotel, as she called the witch, locked her in a high tower in the forest. There were no doors, only a window.

And so, little Rapunzel grew up alone in the tower with only a window at the top. She had the most beautiful, softest hair. Above all, it was exceptionally long and she always wore it in two very long plaits. Whenever the witch wanted to go into the tower, she stood underneath the window and cried: 'Rapunzel, Rapunzel, let down your hair for me'. Then, Rapunzel let down her magnificent long hair and she fastened it with a knot when the witch called. Her hair reached all the way down to the bottom of the tower and the witch climbed up on it. Thus it went day after day, year after year, while Rapunzel tried to forget her solitude by singing.

One day, the king's son was riding through the forest and passed by the tower. He heard a song that was so charming he stopped and listened. He wondered who could have such a sweet, soft voice. When the prince discovered that it was a beautiful girl singing high up in the tower, he wanted to climb up to her, but no entrance was to be found. So he just sat there and listened to the beautiful voice, for days and days. Until one day he saw that a witch came tho the tower, and he heard how she cried, 'Rapunzel, Rapunzel, let down your hair'. Then Rapunzel let down the plaited of her hair, and the witch climbed up to her.

When the witch had left, the prince decided to try his luck. He went to the tower and cried: 'Rapunzel, Rapunzel, let down your hair'. Immediately the hair fell down and the king's son climbed up. At first Rapunzel was frightened, because the witch was the only person she had ever seen. But the prince was very friendly and Rapunzel liked him a lot. He visited her every night after the witch had left and the young couple soon fell in love with each other. He asked her to marry him and she accepted. And every night, the prince brought strands of silk to weave a ladder, with which Rapunzel could escape from the isolated tower.

The young couple would meet every night. The witch knew nothing of the prince's visits, until one day Rapunzel accidentaly let slip while dragging up the weighty witch: 'Tell me, how is it that you are so much heavier for me to pull up than the young king's son?' 'Ah! You wicked child', cried the witch. 'I thought I had kept you apart from all the world, and yet you have deceived me'. In her anger she cut off Rapunzel's beautiful tresses. The witch was so pitiless that she took poor Rapunzel into the desolate wasteland, where the girl had to live in great grief and misery.

Later that day, the witch fastened to the catch of the window the plaits of hair that she had cut off. When the prince came and cried, 'Rapunzel, let down your hair', the witch let the hair down. The prince ascended, but instead of finding his dearest Rapunzel, he found the witch Gotel. She gazed at him with wicked and venomous looks. 'Aha!' she cried mockingly, 'you would fetch your dearest, but the beautiful bird sits no longer singing in the nest. Rapunzel is lost to you and you will never see her again'. The prince became very sad.

The witch Gotel was so angry that she pushed the young boy with all her might out of the window and down the tower. In his fall he grabbed Rapunzel's beautiful long hair that the witch had cut off. The prince landed in some bushes, which broke his fall and saved his life, but thorns pierced his entire body and the light was taken from his eyes. In agonising pain and blinded, the heartbroken prince stumbled away into the forest. Rapunzel's hair had fallen down with the prince, so the wicked witch no longer had a way down from the tower. Now, she was trapped in the tower.

The blind prince wandered about the forest. He ate nothing but roots and berries, and did nothing but weep over the loss of his dearest wife. In this way, he roamed around in misery for many years.

At last he came to the wasteland where Rapunzel lived in wretchedness. She had given birth to twins, a boy and a girl: the prince's son and daughter. With his blind eyes, the prince could not see them. Then he heard the sweetest, softest voice of a mother calling for her two children. Suddenly, that voice seemed very familiar to him and he followed the sound.

The prince went towards the beautiful voice. When he approached, Rapunzel recognised him and fell on his neck. The couple wept for joy and two of her tears wetted his eyes. As if by a miracle, the prince's eyes grew clear again and he could see as before. He embraced his son and daughter. The prince's wanderings and Rapunzel's poverty had come to an end. He led his family to his kingdom where they were joyfully received. And they lived for a long time afterwards, happy and contented.

The End

Hansel and Gretel

Once upon a time, a poor woodcutter lived in a big forest with his two children, Hansel and Gretel, and their cruel stepmother. He worked very hard, but they were still very poor, and often they didn't have anything to eat. One night when the children were in bed, the woodcutter's wife suggested that they go deep into the woods the next day and leave Hansel and Gretel. She hoped the children would be found by someone. It was a hard decision for the woodcutter, but maybe it was the best solution. Hansel and Gretel, who could not sleep because they were so hungry, heard everything. So Hansel thought up a plan.

The next morning, the stepmother woke up Hansel and Gretel. They both got a piece of bread. 'Don't eat it all at once, because it's our last bread', she said. The children carefully put away the bread. While they walked deep into the woods, Hansel secretly threw little white stones out of his pocket. At a spot they had never been to before, the woodcutter made a fire. 'Just lie down and rest, while we go and gather some wood', said the stepmother. 'We'll be back before you know it!' Hansel and Gretel ate their bread. They were so exhausted that they quickly fell asleep.

It was already dark when Gretel woke up and she started crying. She woke up her brother, saying, 'How will we ever get home?' 'Don't be afraid', he comforted her, 'when the full moon shines, we can walk home easily'. Hansel took his sister by the hand and looked around the forest floor in the light of the moon. There was the first stone, and further on, the whole row, shining in the moonlight as if they were silver coins. The children only had to follow the trail. By morning, they were back home. Surprised to see them, their stepmother said, 'Well, you two, we thought we would never see you again!'

A few days later, Hansel and Gretel heard their parents say that they would try to lose them again. Hansel wanted to go out to find more stones, but the door was locked. The next morning they got another piece of bread. Since he didn't have any stones, Hansel used little pieces of bread to mark the way. This time, they went even deeper into the woods, and the children fell asleep again. But when they woke up, all the breadcrumbs had disappeared, eaten by the birds! They walked all night and all the next day, but they couldn't find their way home. Gretel was very brave and didn't cry at all.

Hansel and Gretel didn't have any idea where they were, and on top of that they were very hungry. On the morning of the third day, they saw a little cottage. When they went closer, they could see that the cottage was made completely out of gingerbread. The roof was made of chocolate and the windows were made of sugar. Everywhere they looked, they saw decorations made of candy! The exhausted and hungry children carefully walked closer. They had taken only one bite when they heard someone say: 'Nibble, nibble, gnaw, who is nibbling on my little house?'

Hansel said: 'The wind, the wind, the heaven-sent wind', and went on eating. Suddenly the cottage door opened and an ugly old lady stumbled out. Hansel and Gretel dropped everything because they were afraid. But the lady said kindly: 'Don't be afraid, children, come on in and eat all you can'. She didn't have to say that twice. Hansel and Gretel sat down at the table and ate delicious pancakes with honey and many more sweet things. Afterwards, the lady made two little beds with the softest sheets she had. In a moment, the children fell asleep.

Hansel and Gretel felt like they were in heaven, but the lady who had spoiled them with sweets wasn't at all as nice as she seemed. In fact, she was an evil witch who liked to eat little children! The witch was so old that she couldn't see well anymore, but she could smell children from a long distance. When she smelled Hansel and Gretel nearby, she had rubbed her hands and said to herself: 'These two are mine. I'm not going to let them escape!' The children slept for a long time. The witch was already looking forward to the feast she was about to have. As their faces came out from the blankets, the witch licked her lips. When she saw their rosy cheeks, she thought, 'This will be one of the best meals I've ever had!'

Hansel and Gretel were barely awake when the witch suddenly grabbed the boy. Before he realised what was happening to him, she had already locked him in a shed. There were thick bars on the window and the door was locked. The witch went to Gretel and shouted: 'Go on, you lazy girl, it's about time you did something useful! Make your brother a rich meal, so that he gets nice and fat very soon. As soon as there's some nice flesh on his bones, I'm going to eat him!' Gretel started crying, but she had to do what the witch told her to do. Otherwise, the witch told her, she would eat Hansel that moment!

Gretel worked very hard and barely got anything to eat. But Hansel always got the nicest meals, made by his little sister. In a few days Hansel did get bigger. The witch checked every day to see if Hansel was fat enough to eat yet by feeling his finger through the bars. The clever boy always put a thin chicken bone through the bars, and the old witch couldn't see the difference. She couldn't understand why it was taking so long to fatten him up. He certainly was eating enough. She got impatient and one day, she told Gretel to go and get water to boil her brother in. Gretel was terrified and wanted to save her brother.

The witch was looking forward to her feast. She decided to bake some bread first, as a side dish to go with the boy. While Gretel was making the dough, the witch lit the oven. When the flames flared up, she told Gretel to get into the oven to see if the fire was hot enough. 'But I don't know how to get into the oven', the girl said. 'You silly child, the door is wide enough. Even I can get in!' said the witch. She put her head in the opening to prove it. Gretel didn't waste a second and she gave the witch a big push, shoving her into the oven. As quickly as she could, Gretel closed the door. Her hands shook as she opened the door to the cottage and ran out. She felt terrible but knew she had saved Hansel's life.

Gretel ran to the shed to free her brother. They hugged and laughed and were so happy. Now that the witch was dead, they didn't have to be afraid anymore, so they went back inside the cottage. In the cupboards they found jewellery and diamonds the witch had stolen. 'Much better than my white stones', said Hansel, filling his pockets. They took some more of the candy and left the cottage. A few days later, they found their father's cottage again. He had been very sad without his children and he had sent the stepmother away. Thanks to the witch's treasure, they never had to be hungry again!

The End

Cinderella

Once upon a time, there lived a rich merchant with a beautiful and charming wife. They had a sweet daughter with the fairest blonde hair and blue eyes. One day the mother became very ill and died. The merchant and his daughter were heartbroken. The years passed and the merchant married a widow to look after his beloved daughter. She had two daughters, who were beautiful in appearance but in their hearts, they were dark and ugly. They gave the poor girl all the dirty work to do in the house and because she looked dirty all the time, they called her Cinderella.

One day the king announced a ball, to which all young and beautiful women were invited. From among them, his son, the prince, would choose a bride. When the two stepsisters heard this they called Cinderella: 'Comb our hair, brush our shoes and fasten our buckles, we are going to a wedding feast at the king's castle'.

'Ah,' sighed Cinderella, 'If only I could go to the party...' She begged her stepmother to allow her to go along, but the wicked stepmother laughed and said: 'What! You, Cinderella! You are covered in dust and want to go to a ball? You have no dress or shoes!'

Shrieking, the proud stepdaughters and their mother stepped into a carriage and they left Cinderella behind. The poor girl felt lonely and sad. 'Why can I not go to the ball?' she whispered. 'How can I?' she asked, 'I have no beautiful dress, no shoes. Nothing'.

Cinderella walked outside into the garden to her mother's grave. She had visited it every day since her mother had died, and thought about all the good times that had passed. Tears ran down her cheeks. Then suddenly, she heard a soft, friendly voice: 'Why are you crying?' the friendly voice asked.

It was the sweet voice of her godmother, the beautiful, sweet fairy who had stood at her crib at the time of her birth. Cinderella started crying even harder. 'I'll make sure you can go to the ball', the fairy said. 'That's why I am here'. 'But, but,...' stammered Cinderella between her tears, 'how? I have no dress, nor shoes, I can't..., can't...' she stuttered. 'You have everything and you can have everything', the fairy godmother replied. 'Go to the vegetable garden and fetch the biggest pumpkin you can find'. Surprised, Cinderella did what she had been asked and returned with a huge pumpkin. The fairy waved with her magic wand.

The wand worked magic... Cinderella stood there in a beautiful gown and glass slippers. The pumpkin had turned into a golden coach. 'A coach needs horses', said the fairy. 'Fetch me six mice!' Cinderella ran into the basement and returned with six fat mice. The fairy touched them with her magic wand and they turned into six magnificent grey horses. 'Now we need a rat!' the fairy exclaimed. Cinderella knew that there was living one under the oak tree and with a touch of the wand, it turned into a coachman. 'Now go', said the fairy. 'But be careful: after midnight, the spell will be broken!'

With a gentle whip, the six horses started pulling the coach and galloped in the direction of the palace. At her arrival, the news spread among the guests that an unknown princess of exceptional beauty had turned up. A servant opened the coach door and as if in a dream, Cinderella stepped out. Gracefully, she climbed the long steps. Cinderella entered the ballroom and a silence fell. Everyone was taken by her appearance, including the young prince. He walked up to her. With a graceful nod, he asked her to dance. Cinderella accepted and he gently took her hand.

Soon they whirled across the dance floor. They danced and danced… Both beamed with joy. The other girls watching lost their hopes of becoming the next queen. They saw that Cinderella was the most beautiful and the sweetest of them all. Compared to her, none of them would stand a chance. The king and queen watched the lovely pair and they approved. 'If he is sensible, our son should look no further', the king said. 'She can become princess'. Cinderella had never felt happier and had finally found what she had dreamed of. She forgot her wicked stephmother and her two jealous stepsisters.

Then Cinderella suddenly heard the heavy chimes of the church bell. Oh no! It was almost twelve! Cinderella left the ballroom immediately. She ran down the stairs in her beautiful gown as fast as she could but in her hurry she lost one of her glass slippers. She jumped into her coach, just as the clock struck twelve. Cinderella hurried home. Surprised and abandoned, the poor prince stood on the stairs holding her slipper. He was in love with her. Cinderella arrived just before her stepmother and stepsisters also returned from the ball. She jumped into her bed and pretended to be asleep.

The young prince did not sleep the entire night. He could only think about the lovely princess he had danced with. He asked all his servants whether they knew who she was or where she had gone, but nobody could help him. The next morning the entire country was in uproar. The prince sent a messenger to announce the special news: all the maidens throughout the country had to try on the glass slipper that Cinderella had dropped on the stairs. Whoever the slipper fitted, would become the princess! The prince and his servants were going to travel the entire country to find this mysterious girl.

One day the prince and his entourage arrived in the village where Cinderella lived. He knocked at their door and asked for the young daughters. Of course, the ugly stepsisters wanted to try on the slipper. 'This slipper must and shall fit!' the first stepsister said. 'No it won't', the other yelled. The slipper will fit me!' But the slipper did not fit, and so one of them cut off her toe and the other her heel. But it did not fit! The prince was disappointed. The sisters had sent Cinderella to the kitchen, from where she peeped through the keyhole. She saw how her stepsisters crammed their thick feet into the slipper and chuckled.

The prince heard the laughter of another girl and ordered them to open the door. He waved the girl in. Under the scornful laughter of her stepsisters, Cinderella sat down. She put her slender foot forward, and… the slipper fitted like a glove! The prince looked at the girl and touched her cheek. He recognised the beautiful girl from the ball. 'You will become my bride', he said. The prince put his arms around Cinderella and kissed her. One week later there was a wedding celebration, the like of which the country had never seen. Proudly Cinderella stood in her glass slippers at the altar and she married her prince. They lived happily ever after!

The End

Mother Hulda

Once upon a time, there lived a widow with two daughters. One was pretty, friendly and industrious while the other was ugly, nasty and lazy. And as the ugly one was her own daughter, the widow loved her the most. The pretty one was from the first wife of the widow's dead husband and she was made to do all of the work. Every day the poor girl had to spin until her fingers bled. One day, she saw that her spindle had become marked with blood. Scared that her stepmother would find out, she dipped it into a well to wash it, but it slipped out of her hands and fell in. In her despair, she jumped after it down into the well.

The well was deep and full of water. The girl fell until she reached the bottom. Then, she lost consciousness and did not know for how long she had been lying there. She opened her eyes, she was in a beautiful meadow and the sun was shining on the flowers that grew around her. And she walked through the meadow until she came to a baker's house and oven. Suddenly she heard the bread in the oven call out to her: 'Oh, take me out, take me out or I shall burn. I am baked enough already!' The nice girl didn't hesitate for an instant and with the baker's peel she took out all of the loaves, one after the other.

She walked farther through in the beautiful meadow and into a wood, where she came to a magnificent apple tree. It was weighed down with many juicy apples. Suddenly she heard a voice call out to her: 'Oh, shake me, shake me. My apples are all ripe!' Again the nice girl did not hesitate to follow the tree's wishes. She shook the tree until the apples fell like rain, and she continued until there were no more left to fall. Then she gathered all the fallen apples together in a heap. She strolled farther in the direction of a house.

At last she came to the little house, where an old woman was peeping out from one of the windows. When the girl approached, she saw that the woman had such big teeth that the girl was terrified. As she was about to run away, the old woman called her back: 'What are you afraid of my dear child? I am Mother Hulda. Come and live with me, and if you want to help me with all my work, properly and tidily, things will go well for you. You can stay. You must take great pains to make my bed well and shake it up so thoroughly that its feathers fly about, because when they do it snows in the world above'.

The poor girl told Mother Hulda the story of her wicked stepmother and stepsister and her endless list of work. As the old woman spoke so kindly, the girl took courage, consented and set to work. She did everything to the old woman's satisfaction. She shook the bed with such a will that the feathers flew about like snowflakes.

And so the girl led a good life and never heard a cross word. Every day there was plenty of boiled and roast meat, and she was never hungry again. Mother Hulda praised the girl for her work daily.

After she had lived a long time with Mother Hulda, the girl began to feel sad. Not knowing herself what ailed her, she finally began to think that she must be homesick. Although she was a thousand times better off with Mother Hulda than she had been at home, she still had a great longing to go back. Eventually she said to her mistress: 'I am homesick, and although I am very well off here I cannot stay any longer. I must go back to my own home'. Mother Hulda answered: 'It pleases me greatly that you wish to go home and as you have served me faithfully, I will bring you there!'

She took the girl by the hand and led her to a large door standing open, and as the girl passed through it, a heavy shower of gold fell upon her. The gold hung all about her, so that she was covered in it. 'All this is yours, because you have been so industrious', said Mother Hulda, and as well as that, she returned to the girl the spindle; the very same one that she had dropped down the well. And then the door was closed once more, and the girl found herself back again in the world, not far from her stepmother's house, and as she passed through the yard the cock stood on the top of the well and cried: 'Cock-a-doodle doo! Our golden girl has come home too!'

She went in to see her stepmother, and as she had returned covered with gold she was greeted with joy. The girl told what had happened and when her stepmother heard how the girl had come to have such great riches, she wished that her ugly and idle daughter might have the same good fortune. So she ordered her idle daughter to descend into the well. Soon, the lazy girl found herself at the very bottom and unconscious. As she opened her eyes, she found herself in the same beautiful meadow, and followed the same path her sister had done.

The ugly girl walked through the meadow in the direction of the baker's house. When she came to the baker's oven, the bread cried out: 'Oh, take me out, take me out, or I shall burn. I am quite done already!' But the lazy girl answered: 'I have no desire to blacken or burn my hands. You can stay where you are'. And she went on farther. Soon she came to the apple tree, who called out: 'Oh, shake me, shake me, we apples are all ripe!' But she did not care and answered: 'That is all very well, but suppose one of you were to fall on my head? No, you can stay where you are'. And the ugly girl went on farther.

When she came to Mother Hulda's house she did not feel afraid, as she knew beforehand of her big teeth, and entered into service at once. The first day she put everything into working well. She was industrious and did all that Mother Hulda bade her, because of the gold she expected. But on the second day she began to be idle, and by the third day still more so; Mother Hulda gave her a warning but the next morning she would not even get up. Neither did she make Mother Hulda's bed as it ought to have been made, and did not shake it so all the feathers would fly about. It came that there was no more snow in Siberia, where it is always cold. When Mother Hulda noticed that, she had had enough of the girl and thought it was time for her to go home.

'I will take you back to the world above', Mother Hulda said as she led the girl to the door. The lazy girl stood in the doorway, expecting a shower of gold, and instead a great kettle full of tar was emptied over her. 'That is the reward for your laziness', said Mother Hulda, and shut the door. So the lazy girl came home all covered in tar and the cock on the top of the well on seeing her, cried: 'Cock-a-doodle doo! Our dirty girl has come home too!' And the tar remained stuck fast to her, and never, as long as she lived, could it be got off.

The End

Little Red Riding Hood

Once upon a time, a very long time ago, there was a little girl who lived with her parents in a tiny cottage. The cottage was located in a small village on the edge of the forest. Everybody in the village knew the girl and she was loved by everyone. The whole village looked after her as if she were a precious diamond. Right in the middle of the forest was another sweet little cottage. That was where the girl's grandmother lived. If the girl wanted to visit her grandmother, she had to walk along the path through the forest.

The grandmother, a very kind old lady, loved her granddaughter very, very much. She would have given her anything she could. That's why one day, she decided to make the little girl a wonderful present. It was a red cloak with a red hood to match. The grandmother had the girl come over to try on the cloak, and it fitted perfectly. The cloak looked so nice and the little girl liked it so much, she wore it all the time. Everywhere she went in the village, people called her Little Red Riding Hood. Both the hood and the name suited her very well. She loved to wear it because it reminded her of her grandmother.

But one day something happened. Little Red Riding Hood's grandmother fell ill. Little Red Riding Hood's mother, who had heard the news from the neighbours, baked grandmother a lovely cake and she also made her some fresh butter. Her mother called Little Red Riding Hood and said, 'Maybe you should go and visit grandmother now that she's ill. Take this cake and the fresh butter that I made for her. I'm sure that a visit from you will cheer her up! But you have to promise me to be careful in the forest, because it can be dangerous out there, so don't talk to strangers!' Little Red Hiding Hood promised to watch out and went off down the path through the forest.

Little Red Riding Hood took her basket and made her way through the forest. Not long after she had left the village, Litle Red Riding Hood met a wolf. 'Well, good morning, Little Red Riding Hood. What have you got in the basket you are carrying? And where are you going?' asked the wolf very kindly. 'I have a cake and some fresh butter for my grandmother who is ill and lives in the middle of the forest', said Little Red Riding Hood. The wolf licked his lips and thought 'How I would love to gobble up this little girl. But that's too dangerous here in the woods with all the woodcutters working. What if they see me? But maybe, if I am clever, I can eat her grandmother as well!'

'Well, Little Red Riding Hood', the wolf said, 'what if we both go and visit your grandmother?' Little Red Riding Hood was a sweet and trusting girl, and she saw no harm in the idea. She even thought it would be fun for grandmother to have two visitors. 'OK, that's a good idea', said the little girl. The wolf smiled secretly, for his plan had succeeded. He said: 'I'll race you there, what do you think?' But before Little Red Riding Hood could answer, the bad wolf had already left for her grandmother's cottage. The girl saw some pretty flowers, so she stopped to pick a few to take as a present for grandmother.

The wolf was much faster than Little Red Riding Hood, so he reached grandmother's cottage in next to no time, of course. He knocked on the door and waited for a reply. 'Who is it?' cried poor grandmother from her bed. 'It is only me, Little Red Riding Hood. I've brought you some cake and some fresh made butter!' replied the wolf, in his softest voice. He hoped that grandmother wouldn't know it was him. 'The door isn't locked, my dear, so come right in', the old lady called. The bad wolf bounded in, ran to grandmother's bed as fast as he could and gobbled her right up!

Now the wolf had to hurry, so that he would be ready for Little Red Riding Hood to arrive. The wolf immediately found the old lady's spare nightdress and her nightcap in a drawer, so he put them on as fast as he could, and then closed the curtains to darken the room. He hoped Little Red Riding Hood wouldn't see that he wasn't her grandmother. Then he jumped into grandmother's bed and there he waited for the little girl. Only a few minutes later, Little Red Riding Hood reached her grandmother's cottage. She stood in front of the door and tapped it very gently. She hoped grandmother wasn't sleeping too soundly.

'It's Red Riding Hood. I brought you some homemade cake and fresh butter to make you feel better', the little girl said. The wolf grinned and was already  thinking about eating the little girl. It seemed that his plan was working out just the way he wanted it to. 'Walk right in, dear, the door isn't locked', he croaked, and he was trying to make his voice sound just like grandmother's. 'You sound very strange, grandmother', called Little Red Riding Hood. She wondered what had happened to grandmother's voice. Maybe it was because she was ill that her voice sounded so strange?

'Well, that's because I have a cold, my dear!' the wolf replied. Little Red Riding Hood stepped inside. 'Come over here, so that I can see you', said the bad wolf. Little Red Riding Hood was shocked when she saw her grandmother lying there in her bed. Was it because she was ill and had a cold that she looked so different? Her ears, her eyes, her hands, her mouth – they all looked so strange. 'Why grandmother, what big ears you have!' Little Red Riding Hood said. 'Well, all the better to hear you with!' the wolf cried. Little Red Riding Hood took another good look at her grandmother and said, staring at her: 'Why, grandmother, what big eyes you have!' Grandmother's eyes really did look huge.

'Well, all the better to see you with!' the bad wolf grinned. 'Why, grandmother, what big teeth you have!' the little girl said. 'Well, all the better to EAT you with!' snarled the wolf. And with that, he leapt out of bed. Poor Little Red Riding Hood tried to run away and she screamed at the top of her voice as the wolf tried to grab her and gobble her up. What could she do? She wasn't strong enough at all to fight off the bad wolf. She now realised that he had probably already eaten her grandmother as well! Little Red Riding Hood was really scared. The big bad wolf chased her around the room, trying to catch her!

The only thing that Little Red Riding Hood could do now was to keep screaming and hope that someone would hear her. Luckily, Little Red Riding Hood's father was chopping wood nearby and all of the sudden he heard the little girl's screams. He ran towards the cottage and jumped through the open window. He saw the wolf chasing his little girl and guessed what had happened. The brave man made the wolf spit out grandmother, then raised his axe and chopped him in two. The wolf fell dead and everyone was saved! Thanks to Little Red Riding Hood's father they all lived happily ever after!

The End

The Bremen Town Musicians

Once upon a time, there was a donkey who worked at a mill. For many long years he carried sacks to the mill for his master, a cruel man. Eventually, the donkey's strength began to fail, and as each day came he found himself less capable of work. Then his master began to think of turning him out as cheaply as possible. The donkey, guessing that something was in the wind that did not bode him well, ran away from the place where he had lived for such a long time. And so he decided to take the road to the old city of Bremen; for there he thought he might get a job as a town musician.

When he had gone a little way he found a dog lying by the side of the road panting, as if he had run a long way. 'Now, hold fast! What are you so out of breath about?' said the donkey. 'Oh dear!' said the dog, 'now I am old, I get weaker every day and can do no good in the hunt, so as my master was going to have me killed I have made my escape, but how am I to earn a living now?' - 'I will tell you what', said the donkey, 'I am going to Bremen to become a town musician. You may as well come with me and take up music too. I can play the lute and you can beat the drum'. So the dog agreed and they walked on together.

It was not long before they came upon a cat sitting in the road, looking as dismal as three wet days. 'What is the matter with you, old thing?' said the donkey. 'I would like to know who could be cheerful if her neck was in danger', answered the cat. 'Now that I am old, my teeth are getting blunt and I would rather sit by the oven and purr than run about after mice. My mistress wanted to drown me, so I took myself off. But I do not know what is to become of me'. - 'Come with us to Bremen', said the donkey, 'and become a town musician. You understand serenading'. The cat thought this was a good idea, and went with them accordingly.

The three travellers passed by a yard, where a rooster was perched on the gate crowing with all his might. 'Your cries are enough to pierce bone and marrow', said the donkey, 'what is the matter?' - 'On Sunday morning company is coming, and the mistress has told the cook that I must be made into soup and this evening my neck is to be wrung. So I am crowing with all my might while I can'. - 'You had better come with us', said the donkey. 'We are going to Bremen. You have a powerful voice and when we are all performing together it will have a very good effect'. So the rooster agreed, and all four went on together.

But Bremen was too far off to be reached in one day, and towards evening they came to a wood where they decided to stay the night. The donkey and the dog lay down under a large tree, the cat climbed up among the branches and the rooster flew up to the top, as that was the safest place for him. Before he went to sleep, the rooster looked all around him to the four points of the compass, and saw a little light shining in the distance. He called out to his companions that there must be a house not far off, as he could see a light, so the donkey said: 'We had better get up and go there, for these are uncomfortable quarters'. The dog began to think that a few bones, not quite bare, would do him good.

So they all set off in the direction of the light, and it grew larger and brighter until at last it led them to a robber's house, all lit up. The donkey, being the biggest, went up to the window and looked in. 'Well, what do you see?' asked the dog. 'What do I see?' answered the donkey, 'Here is a table set out with splendid food and drink, and robbers sitting at it and making themselves very comfortable'. 'That would suit us fine', said the rooster. 'Yes indeed, I wish we were in there', said the donkey.

Then they talked together about how they could manage to get the robbers out of the house, until at last they hit on a plan. The donkey was to place his forefeet on the window sill, the dog was to get on the donkey's back, the cat on top of the dog and lastly, the rooster was to fly up and perch on the cat's head. When that was done, at a given signal they all began to perform their own particular music. The donkey brayed, the dog barked, the cat mewed and the rooster crowed.

Then they burst into the room, breaking all the panes of glass in the window. The robbers jumped up when they heard the dreadful sound. They thought they were being attacked by some cruel goblin and they fled into the woods in utter terror. Then the four companions sat down at the table, lavishly piled with food and wine. They made free with the remains of the meal, and feasted as if they had been hungry for a month. They all tasted the different dishes and sang songs. They laughed and laughed at their successful plan and the fleeing robbers. Only when every dish had been finished and the last of the wine drunk, did they go to sleep.

They put out the lights and each sought a sleeping place to suit their nature and habits. The donkey lay down outside under a shelter, the dog preferred a place next to the window, the cat found herself a place on the carpet in front of the warm fireplace and the rooster settled himself on a beam in the eaves of the roof. As they were all tired after their long journey, they soon fell fast asleep. When midnight drew near, and the robbers saw from afar that no light was burning and that everything appeared quiet, their leader said to them that he thought that they had run away without reason, telling one of them to go back and have a look inside.

One of them went back inside and found everything quiet. He went to light a lamp, and mistook the glowing fiery eyes of the cat for burning coals. But the cat flew into his face, spitting and scratching. He cried out in terror and tried to run out, but the dog, who was lying there, jumped at him and bit him on the leg. As he was rushing through the yard by the shelter, the donkey struck out and gave him a great kick with his hind foot, and the rooster, who had been wakened by the noise and felt quite lively, cried out: 'Rooster-a-doodle-doo!'

Then the robber got back as well as he could to his captain, and said: 'Oh dear! In that house there is a gruesome witch, and I felt her breath and her long nails in my face; and by the door there stands a man who stabbed me in the leg with a knife; and in the yard there lies a black spectre, who beat me with his wooden club; and above, upon the roof, there sits the justice, who cried, 'Bring that rogue here!' And so I ran away from the place as fast as I could.' From that time forward the robbers never ventured to that house, and the four Bremen town musicians found themselves so well off where they were, that there they stayed. And the person who last related this tale is still living, as you see.

The End

Sleeping Beauty

Once upon a time there lived a king and queen who were loved by their people. Their happiness was complete when the little princess, Sleeping Beauty, was born. Seven fairies were invited for a visit, but only six of them arrived. Each one of them gave the princess a beautiful gift: one wished for wisdom, another for goodness, and the next beauty. After all the fairies had given their special gifts, someone knocked on the castle gate. They were expecting the seventh fairy, but instead it was a mean witch. She was very angry because she hadn't been invited by the king and the queen.

The witch stood beside the cradle where the innocent little princess was sleeping and shouted a curse: 'When you turn sixteen, you will prick your finger and die!' She laughed wickedly as she left the castle. The king, queen and six fairies were deeply shocked. Luckily the seventh fairy arrived, late as usual. She had wanted to give the princess the skill of drawing, but after the whole drama, she adjusted her wish. The fairy didn't have as much magic as the witch, so she couldn't undo the curse. But she could ease it: the princess wouldn't die, but she would sleep for one hundred years.

The princess started growing, and as the fairies had wished, she grew to be a beautiful, good and smart girl. The king had all the needles and thorns around the castle removed, so that his daughter wouldn't be able to prick herself and make the curse come true. One day, the princess was bored and she wandered through the castle. In the tower she met a servant who was spinning wool into thread. Curious, Sleeping Beauty went closer, because she had never seen a spinning wheel before. 'Would you like to try it?' the lady asked her. Sleeping Beauty sat down behind the wheel and started working. But then it happened! She pricked her finger on the spinning wheel. She fell to the floor sound asleep.

The servant ran down to warn the king and the queen. They poured some water on her face to wake her up again, but Sleeping Beauty didn't open her eyes. The king and queen ordered the best doctors in the country to come to the castle, but even they didn't know what to do. Even magicians and fairies offered their help, but nothing worked. The girl kept on sleeping. In the darkest woods of the kingdom, the witch laughed, finally satisfied. Her plan worked. Sleeping Beauty's life was over and the king and queen were devastated from grief.

Sleeping Beauty was carried to her bed and her mother stood by her, day and night. She worried about the future, when Sleeping Beauty would wake up after a hundred years. There wouldn't be anyone left that she would know or love anymore. How sad that would be! The queen asked one of the seven fairies to come to the castle and told her about her worries. The fairy had a solution: Sleeping Beauty would sleep a hundred years, but, she reminded the queen, the beautiful princess could be awakened by a prince who would truly love her. All it would take to awaken the princess would be a kiss from her prince.

The king and queen were so sad that nobody could comfort them. So, they asked the fairy to make them sleep for a hundred years as well. When they woke, their daughter would wake up and everything would be the same as it had been. The fairy thought it was an excellent idea. She cast a spell, putting the royal family to sleep, along with all the servants, the maids, and the knights as well. The servants had families outside the castle that would miss them for one hundred years.

So the fairy put the whole country to a very deep and peaceful sleep.

The guards fell asleep by the gate; the cooks dropped their spoons and fell asleep at the table. 'When Sleeping Beauty wakes up, everybody will be awake again', the fairy thought. For years there was complete silence in the country. The only sound that could be heard was the wind, the singing of the birds and thousands of people snoring. The clocks kept on ticking at first, but since there was nobody to wind them, they also stopped after a while. The grass kept on growing, trees weren't cut back and bushes covered the walls. Around the castle walls a thick forest grew up. The guards even slept so deeply, butterflies landed on them, thinking they were trees.

And the years went by. A century later a prince was travelling through the country. He lived in another kingdom, but he was very restless. One day he had taken a few of his belongings and had left his country. Without knowing where he was or where he was going, he had found his way to Sleeping Beauty's country. It was difficult for him to lead his horse through the dark forest, but he was happy with this adventure that lightened up his lonely life. The forest seemed endless. Just when he was considering going back, he saw something among the dark trees. The prince had to find out what it was.

The prince pushed the branches aside. It was a castle! He stopped for a moment, but there was no sign of life in or around the castle. He was curious and kept on riding. The bridge was down, but he didn't see any guards. He took a closer look and saw them lying there. They seemed to be dead. Carefully, he continued on his way. There was no noise at all in the castle, and there were more people lying on the floor. Suddenly, he heard one of them snoring. He knew then that they weren't dead, only sleeping. The prince was very puzzled.

The prince shook their shoulders and shouted, but no one woke up. He kept on walking through the silent castle, until he arrived in Sleeping Beauty's room. He saw the pretty girl lying in her bed and his heart jumped in his chest. He stood by the bed for a little while and looked at the girl, with love in his eyes. This was the girl he had been looking for, but had never found before. But she was deeply asleep as well. He took the white hand of the sleeping girl in his own, and gently kissed her hand. At that time, the princess opened her eyes. She looked at the prince and told him she had been waiting a hundred years for him.

The curse was broken. The whole country woke up. They yawned and stretched a bit. The king and queen also woke up and ran immediately to the princess' room. They found her happier and more beautiful than ever before. The king and queen met the prince, who immediately asked for their daughter's hand. The young couple looked at each other with so much love and happiness, that they couldn't refuse. A few days later, cheerful singing and music filled the castle that had been silent for so long. The wedding was beautiful. And Sleeping Beauty lived happily ever after, with her prince!

The End

Snow White

Once upon a time, a long time ago, there were a king and queen who were very happy together and expecting a baby. One day, the queen sat sewing at her window and she pricked her finger with her needle. Three drops of blood dropped on the snow that had fallen on her window frame. She said, 'I hope that our little girl will have skin as white as snow, hair as black as ebony and lips as red as blood'. A few months later the princess was born and she was very pretty. The queen's wishes had come true. The king and queen looked at the lovely baby with her skin as white as snow and together, they decided to name her Snow White.

But their happiness didn't last for long. The queen died soon after Snow White was born. The king was very sad, but he loved his daughter very, very much. They often played together and forgot about their loss for a while. But the king became very lonely. And sometimes Snow White didn't see him for several days, and sometimes she heard him cry behind the thick castle doors. A few years later he met another woman. She was also very pretty. The king was happy again, so that made Snow White happy as well. The king wanted Snow White to have a mother, and he decided to marry again. So from that day on, Snow White had a stepmother.

The new queen was very pretty, but proud and ambitious. She wasn't very nice to Snow White and she hardly spoke to the girl. The queen was also very vain. She owned a magic mirror, which she asked the same question every day: 'Mirror, mirror on the wall, who in the land is fairest of them all?' The mirror always answered the same: 'You, my queen, are fairest of all'. Snow White grew up and became a very pretty young lady, but it wasn't easy for her to live with her vain stepmother. And after her father died, things got really bad. One day the magic mirror said to the queen: 'Queen, you are fair to see, but Snow White is fairer than you'. The evil queen was furious and became very jealous.

The queen was so angry that she decided to get rid of Snow White. Then the queen would be the fairest in the country, nobody else! She ordered a hunter to take Snow White into the woods and kill her. As proof that she was dead, he had to bring Snow White's heart to the queen. The hunter did what he was told and took Snow White to the woods. As he pulled his knife, she started crying and he could not bring himself to kill her. He had always been very fond of Snow White. 'Run away as fast as you can', he told her. Then he killed a deer and took its heart back to the queen. The queen didn't suspect anything and she assumed that she was the fairest again.

Snow White wandered through the woods for many hours, not knowing what to do or where to go. She was exhausted when suddenly she saw a clearing with a tiny cottage in it. She knocked at the door, but nobody answered, so she went inside. There wasn't anybody home, but there was a tiny table with seven tiny chairs around it. There was a big pan on the stove and Snow White was so hungry from her long walk through the woods that she ate a little bit. She had added some herbs from the garden, and it was really good. Afterwards, she cleaned the little kitchen and started to tidy up the rest of the tiny cottage. She had nothing else to do. When everything was clean, she went to take a look upstairs.

Upstairs stood seven tiny beds, all in a row. When she saw the soft sheets, Snow White realised how tired she was after her long journey. She lay down on a few tiny beds and she fell asleep immediately. While Snow White was dreaming, the owners of the cottage came home from work. They were seven dwarves. They were surprised when they saw the tidy kitchen. It was quite messy when they left it that morning. But they were even more surprised when they went upstairs. 'Look, there's somebody sleeping in our beds!' whispered one of the dwarves to the others. She looked so lovely that they all fell silent.

In the morning Snow White woke up, and when she saw the dwarves standing around the bed she was a little bit afraid. 'What is your name?' they asked. They were very nice to her. Snow White told them all about her evil stepmother and what she had done. When the dwarves heard what had happened, they told Snow White that she was welcome to stay with them and that she would be safe in their cottage. Snow White was very grateful. Every day she cleaned the cottage and made a nice meal for the dwarves to eat after a hard day's work in the woods. When the dwarves were away, Snow White had fun playing with the animals in the woods.

Back in the castle, the evil queen still asked her mirror: 'Mirror, mirror on the wall, who in the land is fairest of them all?' And the mirror answered: 'Queen you are fair but Snow White, living over the mountains with the dwarves in the woods is fairest of all'. The queen became very angry and the evil woman thought of a cruel plan: she brewed a poison which she poured over a red apple. If Snow White took one bite of the poisoned apple, she would fall into a deep, deep sleep and never wake up. And then, with Snow White asleep, the queen would always be the fairest of all.

Because she didn't want to make Snow White suspicious, the queen dressed up as an old lady and went to look for the cottage of the seven dwarves. The dwarves had left for work already, cheerfully whistling as always. Snow White was washing the floor when somebody knocked at the door. Snow White was scared, because she still thought that the queen would find her. But it was just an old lady. 'I've got some lovely apples, my dear. Please, take one from me', the old lady said. Snow White looked at the shiny red apple and she took a big bite. As soon as she swallowed it, she dropped to the cottage floor. The queen laughed wickedly and ran back to the castle.

The queen had only just left when the dwarves came home from work. There they found Snow White lying lifeless on the floor by the cottage door. They did all they could to bring her back to life, but nothing worked. They were very sad because they loved Snow White so much. They couldn't part from her and they wanted to see her always, so they made her a crystal coffin, decorated with gold and diamonds. The dwarves put the coffin in a nice place in the woods, not far from their cottage. That way, one of them could always watch over Snow White. The animals of the wood were also very sad about what had happened to their friend and often visited the coffin.

One day a prince came by. He saw the dwarves sitting by the coffin. They told him what had happened to Snow White. When he saw the girl in the coffin, he immediately fell in love with her. He opened the coffin and kissed Snow White. She opened her eyes right away. She saw the prince and knew that she would love him forever. The evil queen couldn't believe what she was hearing when the mirror said, 'Snow White is a thousand times more fair!' The queen choked and died. Snow White and the prince lived happily ever after in the prince's castle. And the seven dwarves? They often came to visit their dearest friends!

The End

Rumpelstiltskin

There once was a miller who was very, very poor, but who had a beautiful daughter. One day he came to speak with the king, and to conceal his poverty he told the king that he had a daughter who could spin gold out of straw. The king was very impressed and said to the miller: 'That is an art that pleases me well. If your daughter is as clever as you say she is, bring her to my castle tomorrow. I will provide her with straw so she can turn it into gold'. And so the next morning, the miller took the poor daughter to the castle of the king, who was desperately in need of money, for his treasure chest was nearly empty.

The girl was brought to the king, who led her into a room that was almost full of straw. He gave her a spinning wheel and spindle, and said: 'Now get to work, and if by the early morning  you have not spun this straw into gold you shall die. I will not be fooled by a poor miller and his daughter'. And he shut the door behind him and left her there alone. And so the poor miller's daughter was left sitting there. She could not think what to do to save her young life. She had no notion of how to set to work to spin gold from straw as her father had promised. As the hours passed her distress grew so great that she began to weep.

All at once the heavy door opened, and in came a little man. 'Good evening, miller's daughter', he said. 'Why are you crying?' 'Oh!' answered the girl, 'I have got to spin gold out of straw, and I don't know how'. Then the little man said: 'What will you give me if I spin it for you?' 'My necklace', said the girl. The little man looked at the necklace, seated himself before the wheel, and whirr, whirr, whirr! Three times round and the bobbin was full. Then he took up another, three times round, and that was full too. And so he went on until the morning, when all the straw had been spun and all the bobbins were full of gold.

At sunrise the daughter gave the little man her necklace and he disappeared. Then she heard the key in the lock of the heavy door. She was sitting next to the pile of gold thread as the king entered. When he saw the gold he was astonished and rejoiced greatly. However, he was not satisfied, because the king was very greedy. He had the miller's daughter taken to another room filled with straw, much more than the night before. 'Girl', he said. 'If you value your life, you must spin it all in one night. If not, you will die. As the king, I cannot afford to be put at a disadvantage by one of my servants'.

The girl did not know what to do, so she began to cry, and then the door opened and the little man again appeared. He said: 'What will you give me if I spin all this straw into gold?' 'The ring from my finger', answered the girl. So the little man took the ring and began once again to send the wheel whirring round, and by the next morning all the straw had been spun into glistening gold. The king rejoiced at the sight, but he could never have enough gold. He took the miller's daughter into a still larger room full of straw and said, 'If you can spin this in one night, you shall be my wife'. For he thought: 'Although she is but a miller's daughter, I am not likely to find anyone richer in the whole world!'

As soon as the girl was alone, the little man appeared for the third time and said: 'What will you give me if I spin the straw for you this time?' 'I have nothing left to give', answered the girl. 'Then you must promise me the first child you have after you are queen', said the little man. She did not know what else to do in the situation, so she promised the little man what he had asked for. He sat down and began to spin. The straw flew through his fingers even quicker than the times before, until all the straw had become gold. Before morning, he had finished. He reminded the girl of her promise and left.

The next morning at sunrise the king came to inspect that all had been done according to his wishes. He was ecstatic when he saw all the gold. 'I think I have enough gold for the moment', he said. 'Later, you can make me some more', but first, we will have a wedding and you will become my queen. From far and near, people came to the biggest wedding the country had ever seen. And so it was that the poor miller's pretty daughter became a queen. A year later she brought a fine child into the world; a little prince. The whole country rejoiced and the queen thought no more of the little man.

One day the little man suddenly came into her room and said: 'Now give me what you promised me: your child'. The queen was terrified, and offered the little man all the riches of the kingdom if he 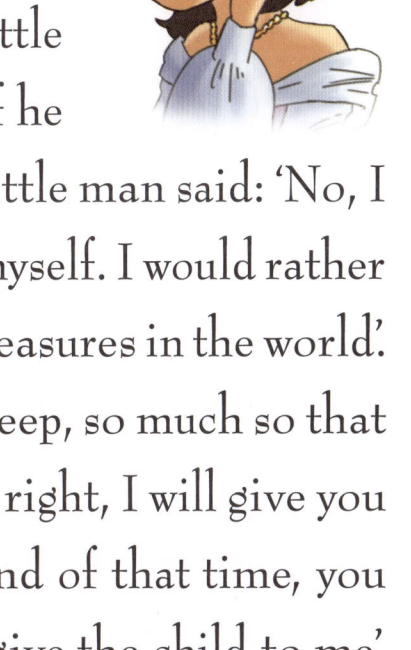 would only leave the child, but the little man said: 'No, I do not want that, as I could make it myself. I would rather have something living than all the treasures in the world'. The queen began to lament and to weep, so much so that the little man had pity upon her. 'All right, I will give you three days', he said, 'and if, at the end of that time, you cannot tell me my name, you must give the child to me'. And the little man disappeared.

The queen then spent the whole night thinking over all the names that she had ever heard. She sent a messenger through the land to ask far and wide for all the names that could be found. And when the little man returned the next day, she repeated all she knew, but after each the little man said, 'That is not my name'. The second day the queen sent to inquire what the servants were called and told the little man all the most unusual and individual names, saying: 'Perhaps you are called Roast-ribs, or Sheepshanks or Spindleshanks?' But he answered nothing, except: 'That is not my name'.

The third day the messenger came back and said: 'I have not been able to find one single new name, but as I passed through the woods I came to a little house, and before the house burned a fire, and round the fire danced a comical little man, and he hopped on one leg and cried:
Today do I bake, tomorrow I brew,
The day after that the queen's child comes in;
And oh! I am glad that nobody knew,
That the name I am called is Rumpelstiltskin!
You cannot believe how pleased the queen was to hear that name!

The third day, the little man walked in and said, 'Now, my Queen, what is my name?' At first, she said: 'Are you called Jack?' 'No', he answered. 'Are you called Harry?' she asked again. 'No,' he answered. And then she said: 'Then perhaps your name is Rumpelstiltskin?' 'The devil told you that!' cried the little man, and in his anger he stamped with his right foot so hard that it went into the ground. Then he stamped his left foot so hard that he disappeared altogether and never came back! After that, the king respected his wife and treated her better from that day onwards. The young prince grew into a kind and brave young man and they all lived as a happy family.

The End